For my aunts Trish and Kathy, two of
my favorite people ever — MF

For my daughter Harper — CS

Text copyright © 2016 by Maureen Fergus
Illustrations copyright © 2016 by Carey Sookocheff
Published in Canada and the USA in 2016 by Groundwood Books
First paperback printing 2018

Groundwood Books / House of Anansi Press
groundwoodbooks.com

We acknowledge for their financial support of our publishing program
the Canada Council for the Arts, the Ontario Arts Council and
the Government of Canada.

Canada Council   Conseil des Arts
for the Arts   du Canada

ONTARIO ARTS COUNCIL
CONSEIL DES ARTS DE L'ONTARIO
an Ontario government agency
un organisme du gouvernement de l'Ontario

With the participation of the Government of Canada | Canadä
Avec la participation du gouvernement du Canada

Library and Archives Canada Cataloguing in Publication
Fergus, Maureen, author
Buddy and Earl go exploring / Maureen Fergus ; pictures
by Carey Sookocheff.
(Buddy and Earl book)
ISBN 978-1-77306-120-7 (softcover).— ISBN 978-1-55498-715-3 (PDF)
I. Sookocheff, Carey, illustrator II. Title. III. Title: Go
exploring. IV. Series: Fergus, Maureen . Buddy and Earl
PS8611.E735B85 2018   jC813'.6   C2017-904261-0

FSC
www.fsc.org
MIX
Paper from
responsible sources
FSC® C012700

The illustrations were done in Acryl Gouache on
watercolor paper and assembled in Photoshop.
Design by Michael Solomon
Printed and bound in Malaysia

BUDDY and EARL go exploring

MAUREEN FERGUS

Pictures by

CAREY SOOKOCHEFF

GROUNDWOOD BOOKS
HOUSE OF ANANSI PRESS
TORONTO   BERKELEY

The day had been long and full of adventures. Buddy was looking forward to a good night's sleep.

Buddy watched Meredith put
Earl into his fancy new home.

He wagged his tail when she and
Michael and Mom and Dad gave
him goodnight hugs and head pats.

Then he scratched his blanket
into a nice messy pile, lay down and
closed his eyes.

All was quiet.
"Goodnight, Buddy," whispered Earl.
"Goodnight, Earl," murmured Buddy.
"Wish me *bon voyage*," whispered Earl.
"*Bon voyage*," murmured Buddy.

"What does *bon voyage* mean, Earl?" asked Buddy.

"It means have a good trip," replied Earl.

"I did not know you were going on a trip," said Buddy.

"It was a spur-of-the-moment decision," admitted Earl.

"Where will you go?" asked Buddy.

"Wherever the road leads me," replied Earl.

"How long will you be gone?" asked Buddy.

"However long it takes," replied Earl.

This answer worried Buddy.

What if whatever *it* was took a long time?

What if *it* took forever?

He might never see Earl again!

Even though his big heart was almost breaking, Buddy
tried to be brave.

"Goodbye, Earl!" he cried. "Good luck!"

Earl solemnly saluted his friend.

Then he climbed onto his wheel and started running.

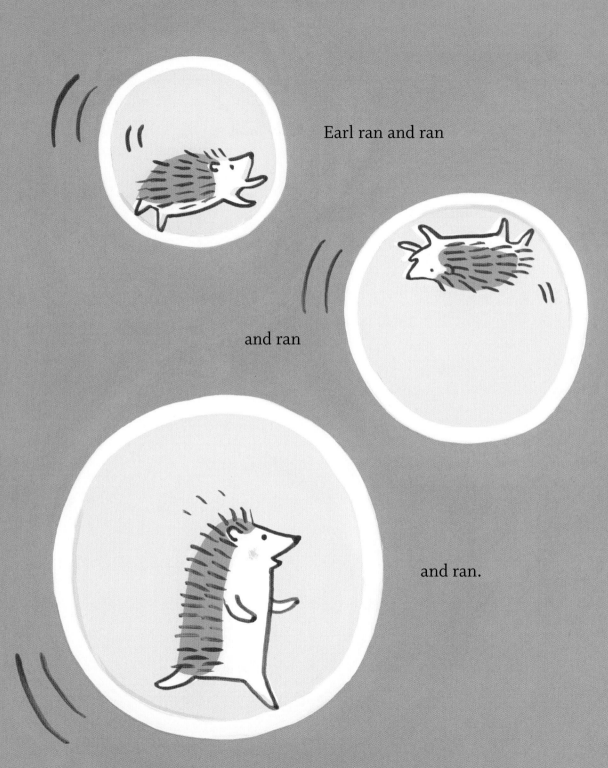

Earl ran and ran

and ran

and ran.

After a long time, he stopped and
looked around.

"This place looks eerily similar to
the place I just left," whispered Earl.

"Maybe that is because it *is* the place you just left," whispered Buddy.

When he heard Buddy's voice, Earl was so startled that he jumped and made a funny popping sound.

"I ran faster than the wind!" he cried. "How did you manage to keep up with me, Buddy?"

"I am not sure," said Buddy uncertainly.

"Well, I'm glad you're here," declared Earl. "Exploring is always more fun if you do it with a friend."

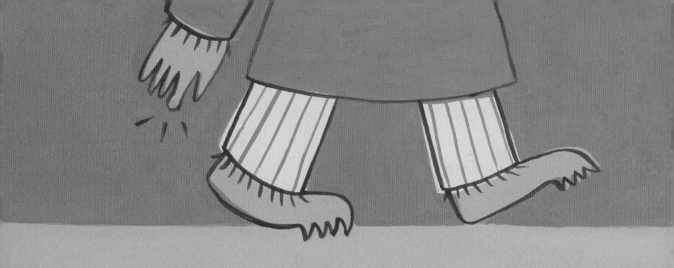

"We'll have to explore quietly," said Earl. "Otherwise, the hideous ogre will hear us."

"What hideous ogre?" asked Buddy in alarm.

"The one with the glasses and the ugly blue housecoat," said Earl. "The one that makes such a racket when you bite it as hard as you can."

"The hideous ogre sounds a lot like Dad," said Buddy.

"I know," said Earl with a shiver. "Let's go!"

They hadn't gone far before Earl saw something amazing.

"Look, Buddy — a silvery lake in the shadow of a great mountain!" he exclaimed.

"That is my water dish in the shadow of the garbage pail," said Buddy.

"Last one in is a rotten egg!" whooped
Earl as he waddled over and climbed into
the lake.

Earl floated and splashed and kicked.
"Come on in, Buddy!" he called. "The
water is beautiful!"

Filled with excitement, Buddy bounded toward the water dish.
Unfortunately, he ran into a little trouble along the way.

Buddy felt terrible about knocking over the garbage can.

Then he noticed some of yesterday's meatloaf and forgot all about feeling terrible.

When Earl saw that it was snack time, he hurried to join in.

Earl had just discovered a half-eaten carrot when he gasped and pointed at something in the distance.

"What is it, Earl?" asked Buddy anxiously. "What do you see?"

"I see a lovely lady hedgehog trapped in the jaws of a monster!" cried Earl.

"That is not a lady hedgehog and a monster, Earl," said Buddy. "That is Mom's hairbrush and purse."

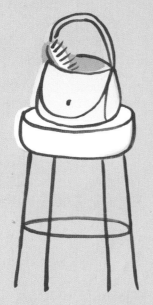

"I WILL SAVE YOU, MY DARLING!" bellowed Earl as he charged across the room.

Earl tried to grab the monster, but it was no use.

"You have to attack the monster for me, Buddy," panted Earl.

"I am not supposed to attack Mom's purse, Earl," said Buddy.

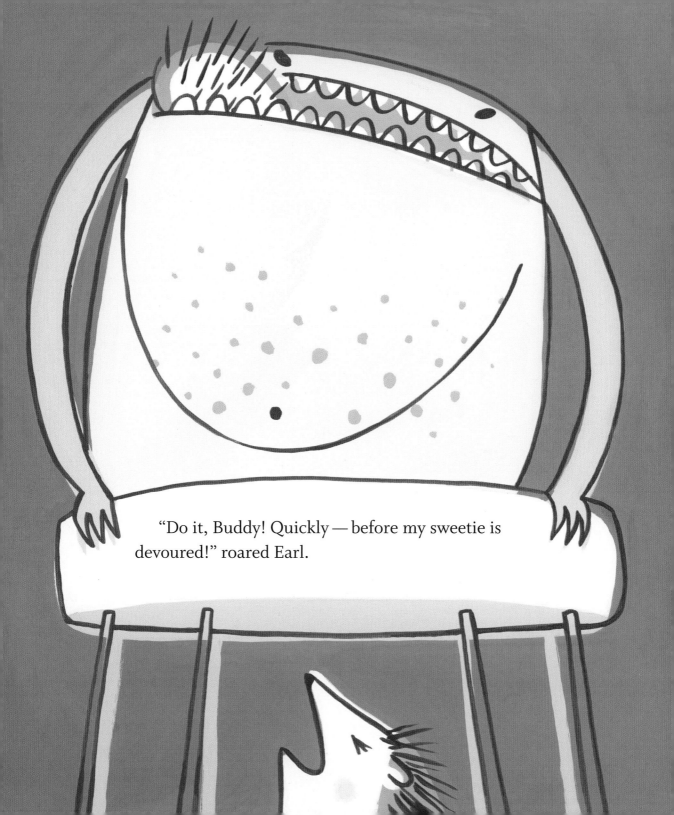

"Do it, Buddy! Quickly — before my sweetie is devoured!" roared Earl.

Buddy did not want Earl's sweetie to be devoured, so he gave the purse strap a mighty yank.

Mom's purse toppled off the stool.

Earl's sweetie was saved!

Earl gave Mom's hairbrush his most charming smile.

"Do you think she likes me, Buddy?" he whispered.

Buddy couldn't answer because
he had just caught sight of *another*
monster: THE VACUUM CLEANER.

Buddy was very scared.

Luckily, Earl came to the rescue.

Glaring up at the monster, he shouted, "Attack, and I *will* prickle you!"

Instead of roaring to life and gobbling up Earl, the vacuum cleaner just stood there.

Buddy was saved!

"You are my hero, Earl!" cried Buddy.

"And you are my hero, Buddy," said Earl. "And do you know what else? I think we've done enough exploring for one night."

Buddy helped Earl back into his home, then lay down and closed his eyes.

"*Bon soir*, Buddy," murmured Earl.

"Oh, no," said Buddy. "What does *bon soir* mean, Earl?"

"It means goodnight," replied Earl.

"Oh," sighed Buddy happily. "Well, then — *bon soir*, Earl. Goodnight."